Contents

*Levels**	*Title*	*Composer*	*Page*
G S	**Ice Skateboarding**	Adam Gorb	2
G (S)	**The Lonely Girl Sings**	Colin Cowles	3
G (S)	**Londonderry Air**	Trad. arr. Nigel Scaife	4
G G	**The Secret Garden**	Pam Wedgwood	5
G G	**Minor Variations**	Alan Haughton	6
G (P)	**Tarantella!**	Paul Harris	7
G G (S)	**The Trout**	Schubert arr. Paul Harvey	8
G G G	**September Sunset**	Barrington Pheloung	10
G G G	**The Lass of Richmond Hill**	James Hook arr. Robert Hinchliffe	12
G G (P)	**The Big Dipper**	Paul Harris	14
G (S) (S) (S)	**Andante** from Symphony No. 3, Op. 90	Brahms arr. Mark Goddard	16
G G G (S)	**Jambular**	Pam Wedgwood	18
G G P P	**Holiday Rag**	Alan Haughton	20
G G G P	**Cornish Dance**	Paul Harris	22

*S = silver; G = gold; P = platinum; ( ) = the line must be played but cannot be assessed for a Medal.

Ice Skateboarding

Adam Gorb

The Lonely Girl Sings

Colin Cowles

Londonderry Air

Trad. arr. Nigel Scaife

The Secret Garden

Pam Wedgwood

Minor Variations

Alan Haughton

Tarantella!

Paul Harris

for Ella

The Trout

Schubert arr. Paul Harvey

13
p
mf

17
mf
p

21
p

September Sunset

Barrington Pheloung

12
f
mp
f
mp
f
mp

16
mf
mp
p
mf
mp
p
mf
mp
p

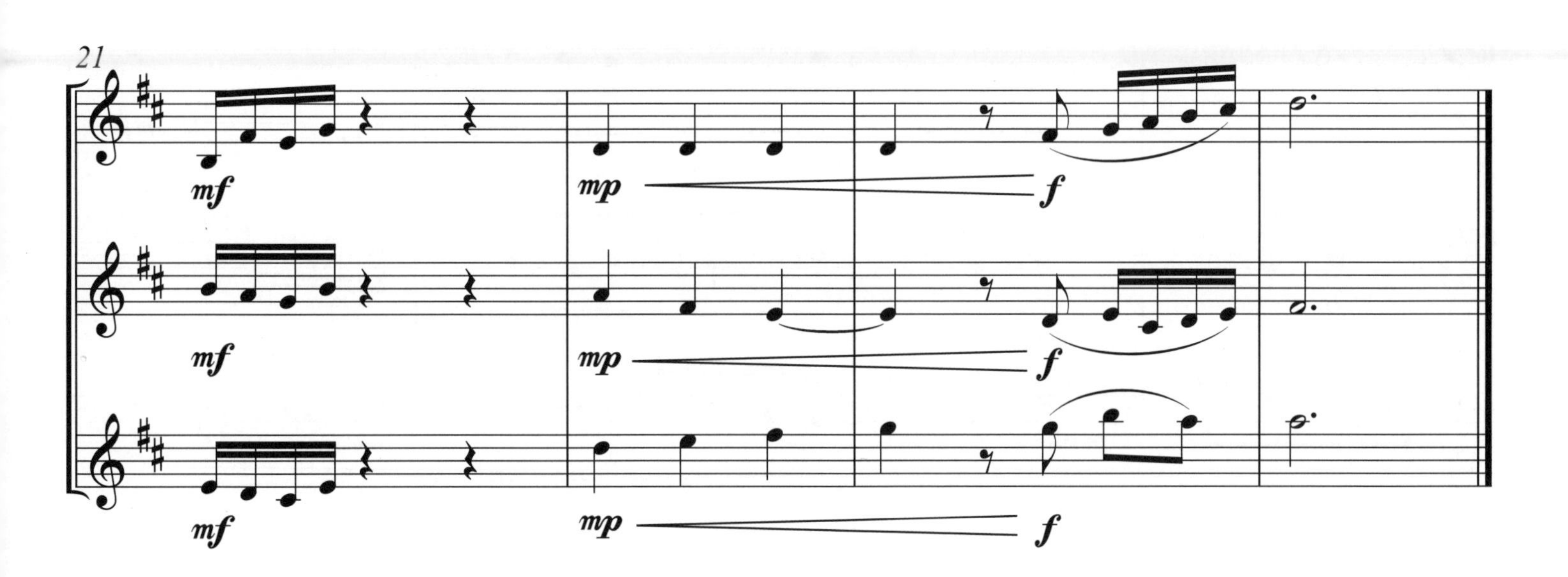
21
mf
mp
f
mf
mp
f
mf
mp
f

The Lass of Richmond Hill

James Hook arr. Robert Hinchliffe

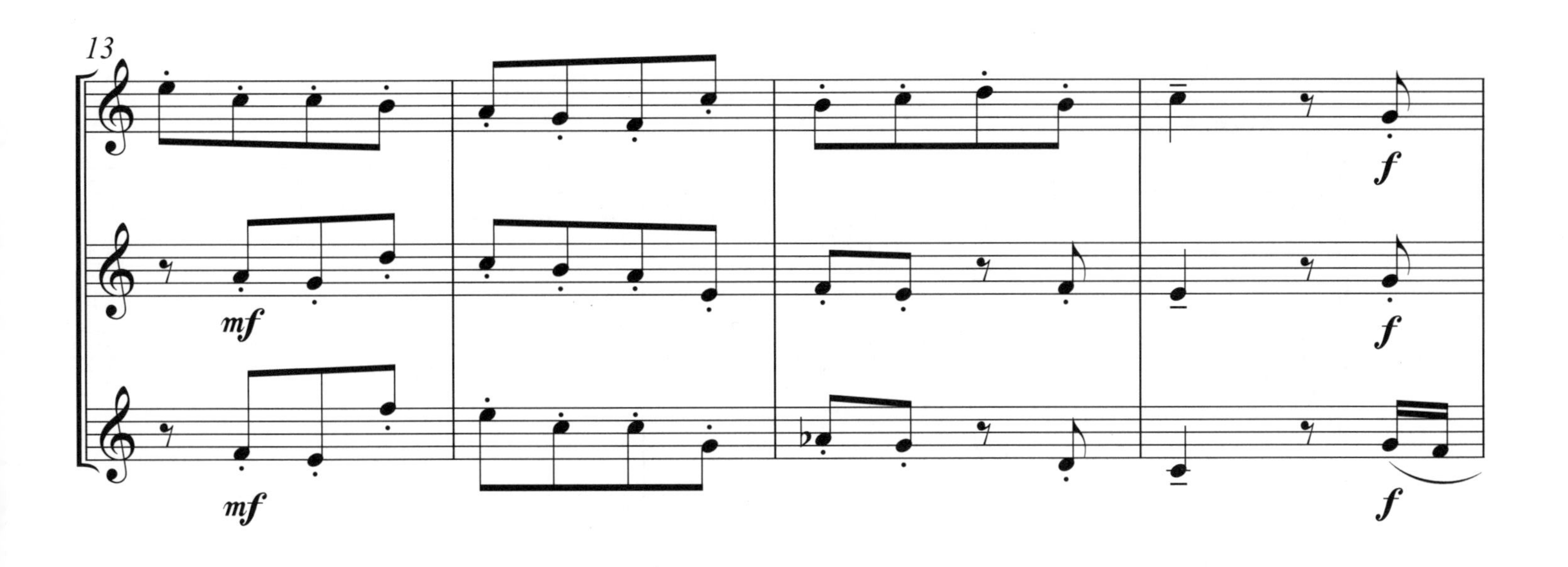
13
mf
mf
f
f
f

17

21

The Big Dipper

Paul Harris

15
mf
mf
3
mf

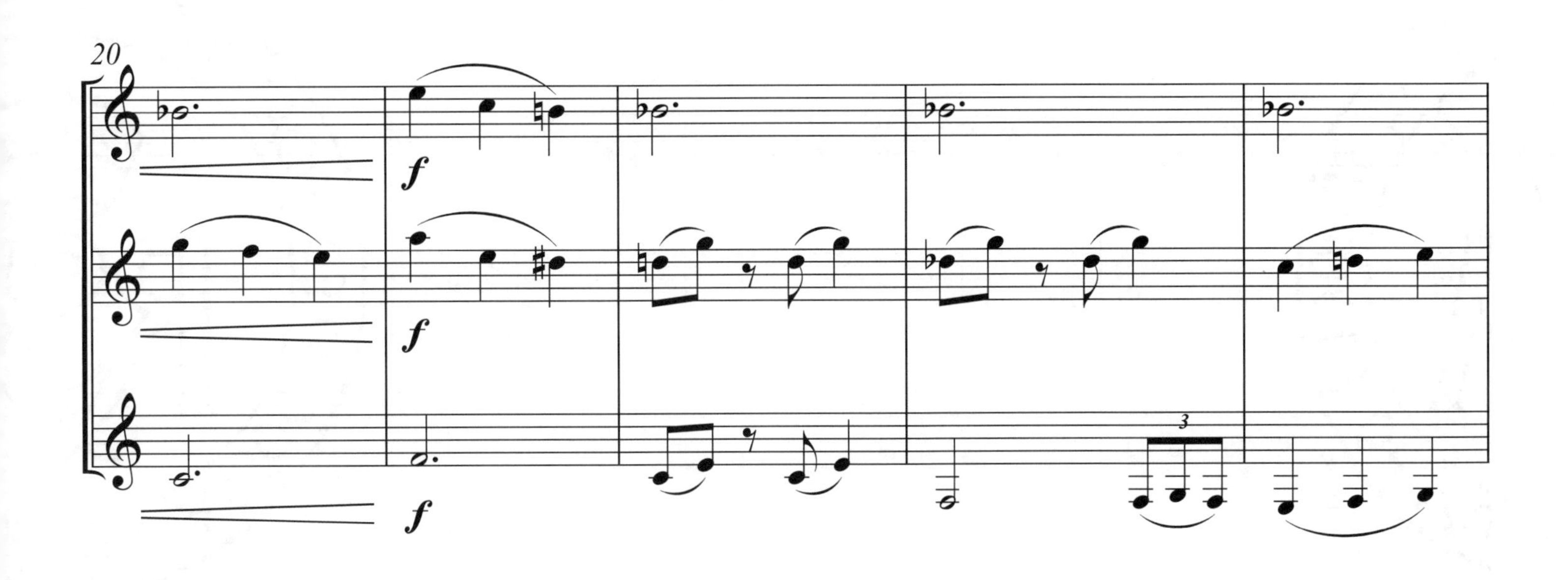
20
f
f
3
f

25
mf
f
mf
f
mf
f

Andante

from Symphony No. 3, Op. 90

Brahms arr. Mark Goddard

13

17
pp
pp
pp
pp

Jambular

Pam Wedgwood

13
mf
mf
mf
mf
17
f
f
f
f
22
mp
f
mp
f
mp
f
mp
f

Holiday Rag

Alan Haughton

10
f
f
f
f
13
mp
mp
mp
mp
17
f
f
f
f

Cornish Dance
music medals
Paul Harris
Moderato ma molto energico ♩ = c.84
gold 1
gold 2
gold 3
platinum 4
f
mf
3

11
p
p
p
p
15
f
f
f
f
3
3
3
3
18
3
3
mf
mf
mf
mf

21
p cresc.
mf
p cresc.
mf
p cresc.
mf
p cresc.
mf

25
f
f
f
f

28
ff
ff
ff
ff